EGMONT

We bring stories to life

First published in Great Britain 2012 by Dean,
an imprint of Egmont UK Limited
239 Kensington High Street, London W8 6SA

HiT entertainment

ISBN 978 0 6035 6677 6
51289/1
Printed in China

Twist of Fate

One afternoon, the Fire Crew were busy doing jobs around the Fire Station.

Penny was using a grease gun to oil Jupiter's squeaky wheel. But when Elvis picked it up, he accidentally squirted himself in the face!

"Elvis, just look at your face," said Fireman Sam, arriving with some rescue equipment. "You'd better get cleaned up. We can't let standards drop just because Station Officer Steele is away."

Station Officer Steele wasn't at the Fire Station, as he was taking Norman and Mandy pot-holing in Pontypandy Big Cave.

Norman was very excited, as he'd just heard on TV that there was gold in the Welsh hills!

Dilys put some sandwiches in Norman's rucksack.

"Thanks Mam, I'll bring you back some gold if I find any," Norman said, as he set off with Station Officer Steele and Mandy.

Dusty sniffed at Norman's rucksack as he left.

The explorers arrived at the opening to Big Cave.

"Have we got everything we need?" asked Station Officer Steele.

"I've got my turkey sandwiches!" giggled Norman.

"Don't be cheeky. I mean our hard hats, ropes, headlamps and spare batteries," said Station Officer Steele, giving Norman the batteries.

"All present and correct, sir!" replied Norman, putting the batteries in his rucksack.

But Norman didn't realise there was a hole in the bottom of his bag!

Norman was about to enter Big Cave when Station Officer Steele stopped him.

"I'll go first," said Officer Steele. "Remember, stick with me at all times and don't wander off down any side passages . . ."

Station Officer Steele disappeared into the cave.

"Go with a grown-up who knows what he's doing," he continued, as Mandy and Norman followed behind.

Just then, the spare batteries fell through the hole in Norman's rucksack!

In Big Cave, Norman spotted something.

"Look, there's a secret underground passage," cried Norman. "I can see something shiny!"

Officer Steele reluctantly followed Norman and Mandy into the small gap. The passage got narrower, and then Norman and Mandy crawled through a small hole.

Station Officer Steele started to follow them through the hole, then he let out a cry.

"Oh no! Help me, I'm stuck!" he shouted.

Norman and Mandy tried to hide their giggles.

"It's no laughing matter!" said Officer Steele. "I'm blocking the only way out!"

In the village, Dilys was getting worried. Norman hadn't come back from pot-holing yet.

She phoned the emergency services to report him as a missing person.

The message went straight through to the Fire Station where Fireman Sam picked it up.

"Oh no! Norman's not home yet," he cried. "It's almost 5 o'clock. Action Stations, everyone!"

Quick as a flash, Jupiter was racing to Big Cave with Nurse Flood on board.

Nee Nah! Nee Nah!

In Big Cave, Station Officer Steele was still stuck in the hole. Suddenly, Norman's light went out!

"It must be the battery. Pop in one of the spares I gave you," said Station Officer Steele.

Norman rummaged in his rucksack. "They must have fallen out!" he gasped.

Just then, Mandy's light went out, too.

"The important thing is not to panic," said Station Officer Steele. "I'm sure Fireman Sam is already looking for us. Let's sing, so they can hear us."

Fireman Sam and Nurse Flood were searching Big Cave. But they couldn't find the explorers, and they were worried they might be hungry.

"That's it! Sandwiches!" said Sam suddenly.

He had an idea. Moments later, Dusty was with them, barking excitedly at the cave entrance.

"Dusty can smell meat a mile off, so he should find Norman's turkey sandwiches," said Fireman Sam.

Dusty pulled on his lead, dragging Sam through Big Cave with Nurse Flood following behind.

In the cave, Station Officer Steele, Norman and Mandy were still singing. Suddenly, they heard cries in the distance.

"Mandy! Norman! Station Officer Steele!" cried Fireman Sam.

"Shhh, listen," said Station Officer Steele. "Children, I want you to make as much noise as possible."

Sam and Nurse Flood were racing after Dusty. Then they heard the explorers' voices echoing in the distance.

Soon, Dusty found Station Officer Steele and tried to scramble past him to the sandwiches!

"Get that dog off me," said Station Officer Steele.

"Don't worry! We'll soon get you free!" said Sam. But despite their attempts, he wouldn't move.

"We need something slippery and I know just the thing," said Sam, phoning Penny.

In no time, Penny arrived with the grease gun and Fireman Sam set to work squirting it around Station Officer Steele's waist.

Moments later, Sam stepped back, taking one of Officer Steele's legs as Penny took the other.

"On the count of three . . . pull. One . . . two . . . three," said Sam.

The pair pulled Station Officer Steele's legs until he was free of the hole and safely on the ground.

"Hurray for Fireman Sam!" cheered Norman, as Sam's head popped through the hole.

"It's all right now, everything's OK," said Sam, as Dusty went straight for Norman's sandwiches.

Fireman Sam, Norman, Mandy and Nurse Flood travelled home in Jupiter.

"Next time, listen to Station Officer Steele," said Sam. "And don't lose your spare batteries."

"OK, we'll listen next time," replied Norman. "You know, we never did find any treasure."

"Well, we did find Dilys' little treasure . . . you!" said Sam.

And everyone laughed, except Norman!